This ELMER book belongs to:

. . . .

For Bryony and Leonie

This paperback edition first published in 2009 by Andersen Press Ltd.
First published in Great Britain in 1994 by Andersen Press Ltd.,
20 Vauxhall Bridge Road, London SW1V 2SA.
Copyright © David McKee, 1994
The rights of David McKee to be identified as the author and illustrator
of this work have been asserted by him in accordance with the
Copyright, Designs and Patents Act, 1988.
All rights reserved.
Colour separated in Switzerland by Photolitho AG, Zürich.
Printed and bound in Malaysia by Tien Wah Press.

10   9   8   7   6   5

British Library Cataloguing in Publication Data available.

ISBN 978 1 84270 950 4 (Trade paperback edition)
ISBN 978 1 84270 983 2 (paperback and CD edition)

This book has been printed on acid-free paper

ELMER
and Wilbur

David McKee

Andersen Press

Elmer, the patchwork elephant,
was waiting for his cousin, Wilbur,
who was coming to visit him.
"He's late," said Elmer. "Perhaps he's
lost. Let's go and look for him."

"What does Wilbur look like?" asked an elephant.

"Wait and see," chuckled Elmer. "But be careful, Wilbur likes to play tricks, especially with his voice. He's a ventriloquist. He can make his voice sound as if it is coming from a different place to where he is, from anywhere."

"This is fun," said an elephant as they started to search. "It's like hide-and-seek."

Suddenly they heard, "Yo Ho! Elmer! I'm over here."
They rushed to where the voice came from.
"Looking for me?" asked a rather surprised tiger.
"Sorry," said Elmer, "we thought you were my cousin."
"Very funny, Elmer," said the tiger. "Perhaps
that's your cousin I can hear shouting."

"Help!" called the voice. "Help! I've fallen in the pond."

"He has, he has! I can see him!" said an elephant.

"Silly," said Elmer. "That's your own reflection. Keep looking. He's near, but not where his voice is."

They kept looking and all the time they looked, the voice came from different places. It called, "COOEEE! Here I am," or "BOO!" to make them jump. It even came from down a rabbit hole. The rabbits popped out, saying, "That's not funny. That's not funny at all. That's very silly."

After a lot of searching, an elephant said,
"We'll never find him, Elmer. Let's give in."
"Wilbur," called Elmer. "We give in. You can
come out now."
"I can't. I'm stuck up a tree," Wilbur's voice said
from above them. The elephants giggled. "He's
very clever," said one.

"If you don't come," said Elmer, "we'll have to go home without you."

"I really am stuck up a tree," said Wilbur's voice. The elephants giggled again.

"Elmer," said an elephant. "Is Wilbur black and white?"

"Yes. Why?" said Elmer.

"I peeped," said the elephant. "He really is stuck up a tree."

They all looked.
There was Wilbur, up a tree.
"Wilbur," gasped Elmer. "How did you
get up there?"
"Never mind how I got up, how do
I get down?" said Wilbur.

"I've no idea," said Elmer. "But we're hungry so we're going home for tea. At least we know where you are now. Goodbye, Wilbur. See you tomorrow."

With that, Elmer started to lead the other elephants away.
"Oh, Elmer," called Wilbur. "Don't leave me. I'm starving."

"Ha, ha, I was just teasing,"
laughed Elmer, turning back to Wilbur.
"If you walk along the branch it will bend down
with your weight and we can help you down."
Wilbur walked slowly along the branch. The branch
began to bend down. When the elephants could
reach, they pulled the branch the rest of the way
and helped Wilbur off.

"Thanks," said Wilbur. "Now, where's that tea you were talking about?" Then laughing and joking together they raced all the way home.

That night, as they lay down to sleep, Elmer said,
"Goodnight, Wilbur. Goodnight, Moon." A voice that
seemed to come from the moon said, "Goodnight,
elephants. Sweet dreams."

Elmer smiled and whispered, "Wilbur, how DID you get up that tree?" But Wilbur was already asleep.